For Amara and Leela.
Thank you for always asking the right questions.
—MH

For Ms. Shearburn, Ms. Roberts, and Ms. Bean.
Thank you for helping me find my way forward.
—KM

ABOUT THIS BOOK

The illustrations for this book were done with tissue paper collaged in Adobe Photoshop. This book was edited by Farrin Jacobs and designed by Saho Fujii and Camryn Cogshell. The production was supervised by Kimberly Stella, and the production editor was Jen Graham. The text was set in Archer Medium, and the display type was hand lettered by Alanna Flowers.

Text and illustrations copyright © 2022 by Meena Harris • Illustrations by Keisha Morris • Cover illustration by Keisha Morris • Hand lettering © 2022 by Alanna Flowers • Cover design by Camryn Cogshell and Patrick Collins • Cover copyright © 2022 by Hachette Book Group, Inc. • Hachette Book Group supports the right to free expression and the value of copyright. The purpose of copyright is to encourage writers and artists to produce the creative works that enrich our culture. • The scanning, uploading, and distribution of this book without permission is a theft of the author's intellectual property. If you would like permission to use material from the book (other than for review purposes), please contact permissions@hbgusa.com. Thank you for your support of the author's rights. • Little, Brown and Company • Hachette Book Group • 1290 Avenue of the Americas, New York, NY 10104 • Visit us at LBYR.com • First Edition: October 2022 • Little, Brown and Company is a division of Hachette Book Group, Inc. • The Little, Brown name and logo are trademarks of Hachette Book Group, Inc. • The publisher is not responsible for websites (or their content) that are not owned by the publisher. • Library of Congress Cataloging-in-Publication Data • Names: Harris, Meena, author. | Morris, Keisha, illustrator. • Title: The truth about Mrs. Claus / by Meena Harris ; illustrated by Keisha Morris. • Description: First edition. | New York ; Boston : Little, Brown and Company, 2022. | Audience: Ages 4–8. | Summary: "Amalia is not sure she is meant to be a teddy-bear-making elf and seeks out Santa for advice, only to discover a secret about Mrs. Claus." —Provided by publisher. • Identifiers: LCCN 2021031460 | ISBN 9780316232272 (hardcover) • Subjects: CYAC: Elves—Fiction. | Problem solving—Fiction. | Ability—Fiction. | Santa Claus—Fiction. | LCGFT: Picture books. • Classification: LCC PZ7.1.H37469 Tr 2022 | DDC [E]—dc23 • LC record available at https://lccn.loc.gov/2021031460 • ISBN 978-0-316-23227-2 • Printed in the United States of America • PHX • 10 9 8 7 6 5 4 3 2 1

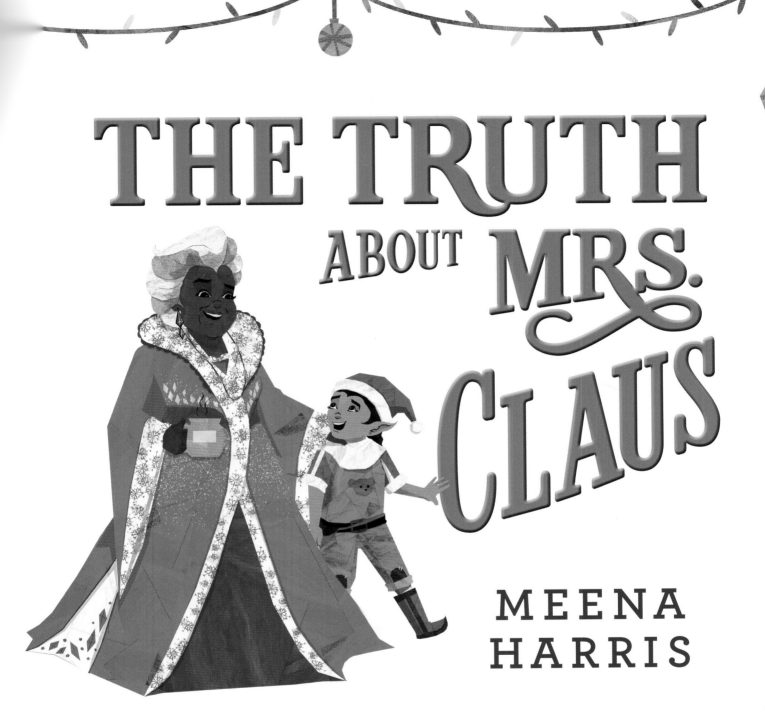

THE TRUTH
ABOUT MRS.
CLAUS

MEENA
HARRIS

Illustrated by **KEISHA MORRIS**

L B

LITTLE, BROWN AND COMPANY
New York   Boston

Amalia the Elf came from a long line of proud teddy-bear makers. A very long line.

Great-Grandma's bears were the fluffiest in the whole North Pole.

Grandma's bears had the smoothest satin bows.

Mama's bears glinted with the shiniest golden stitches.

Amalia was getting good at making bears, too.
Last Christmas, Santa had even given her the Most
Imaginative Bear Maker Award!

MOST
IMAGINATIVE
BEAR MAKER!

"Lovely bows," said Grandma.

"Beautiful stitches," said Mama.

"Well done, Amalia," they both said.

But no matter how hard she tried . . . making bears didn't make Amalia happy.

Amalia did love the smell of stuffing and the feel of velvety fur. She loved watching Grandma's fingers glide over the satin, and how Mama's eyes sparkled as she guided the needle and golden thread.

And she really loved telling stories about where each bear might live someday.

"This one is going to soar across the sky with Santa, all the way to a sandy shore. She'll find a home with a girl who loves to surf, and they'll build the biggest sandcastle in the world!

"This one will live in the mountains with a boy who loves to climb trees all day, and at night they'll sleep under a blanket of stars."

The truth was, Amalia loved everything about being a bear-making elf . . .

. . . except the bear-making part. But she didn't want to disappoint Mama and Grandma. Bear making was what their family did!

Amalia needed advice. And there was only one person she could think of to help her.

She headed out in the early-morning light to find Santa.
The snow crunched beneath her feet. The tinsel trees whispered
above her head. Suddenly, a flash in the sky caught her eye—
a sleigh!

Amalia watched it skim
the twinkling treetops and
glide to a stop in front of
Santa's Workshop.

She saw a figure
speak softly to the
reindeer before
striding inside.

This was her chance. Amalia scurried after the figure . . .

following him through the Wrapping-Paper Room . . .

past the Candy-Cane Tasters . . .

all the way through an open office door.

"Santa?" she said bravely.

"*Mrs.* Claus?!" Amalia hung her head. "You're not Santa."

"I'm not," said Mrs. Claus. "Do you need him for something?"

"Yes," said Amalia. "I'm having a bear-making problem."

"Oh, that sounds serious." Mrs. Claus paused. "Good thing you found my office."

"*Your* office?"

"Yep. Now, maybe I can help with your bear-making problem."

"Will Santa be back soon?" Amalia asked.

"I'm sure he's around somewhere. In the meantime, come with me, and I'll tell you a story."

"I love stories," said Amalia.

Mrs. Claus smiled. "This one is very special. It's about a young woman named Sarah B. Claus. . . .

"When I first came to the North Pole, I did what I thought Mrs. Claus was supposed to do: bake cookies, serve cookies, and bake more cookies. Don't get me wrong—I like baking, and my holiday cookies are fantastic. But I wanted to do more.

"So I went all over the Workshop and learned every last detail and task: what materials you need to make each toy, the best tips for training reindeer, even how to drive—and fix—Santa's sleigh. And each year, with my ideas and suggestions, Christmas ran more and more smoothly. I realized that what I really enjoyed was making sure the North Pole was working the best it possibly could!"

"What about Santa?"

"He has his job," Mrs. Claus said with a smile, "and I have mine."

"Wow, Mrs. Claus! I had no idea you did all this."

"How could you have known?" Mrs. Claus looked closely at Amalia. "The point is that I found what I love to do," she said, "and you'll figure out what you love to do, too."

"How did you know I don't love making bears?" Amalia asked.

"I had a feeling when Santa gave you the Most Imaginative Bear Maker Award," said Mrs. Claus. "Making bears didn't seem to excite you, but making up stories about them lit up your face!"

"Can you help me, Mrs. Claus?" Amalia asked. "I want to make my family proud, but if I'm not a bear-making elf like them, who am I?"

"That's a hard question, Amalia," said Mrs. Claus. "But it's also an exciting one. This is your chance to discover your destiny and to find what you love. It's your chance to tell your own story!"

Amalia was quiet a moment. Then she asked,

"So why is your story a secret?"

"Well," said Mrs. Claus, "people think Christmas is run by Santa and the elves. That's how the story goes. That's how it's always been."

"But maybe that's not how it should be!"

Amalia thought about Mama and Grandma and how they'd never seen Amalia do anything other than bear making.

"Maybe people only believe what they see, so we have to *show* them who we are."

Mrs. Claus looked surprised. "What a clever elf you are," she said. "I guess I never thought anyone needed to know."

"Mrs. Claus, *I* needed to know," said Amalia. "And I'm sure I'm not the only one."

Mrs. Claus took a deep breath. "Some people probably won't *want* to know the truth. But if you think it could help others . . .

". . . I'm going to need someone to tell my story."

Amalia the Elf came from a long line of teddy-bear makers. A long line that was changing with every generation.

Great-Grandma's bears were the fluffiest in the whole North Pole.

Grandma's bears had the smoothest satin bows.

Mama's bears glinted with the shiniest golden stitches.

And Amalia's bears—they left the North Pole with the best stories under their arms.

And Amalia was ready to write more.

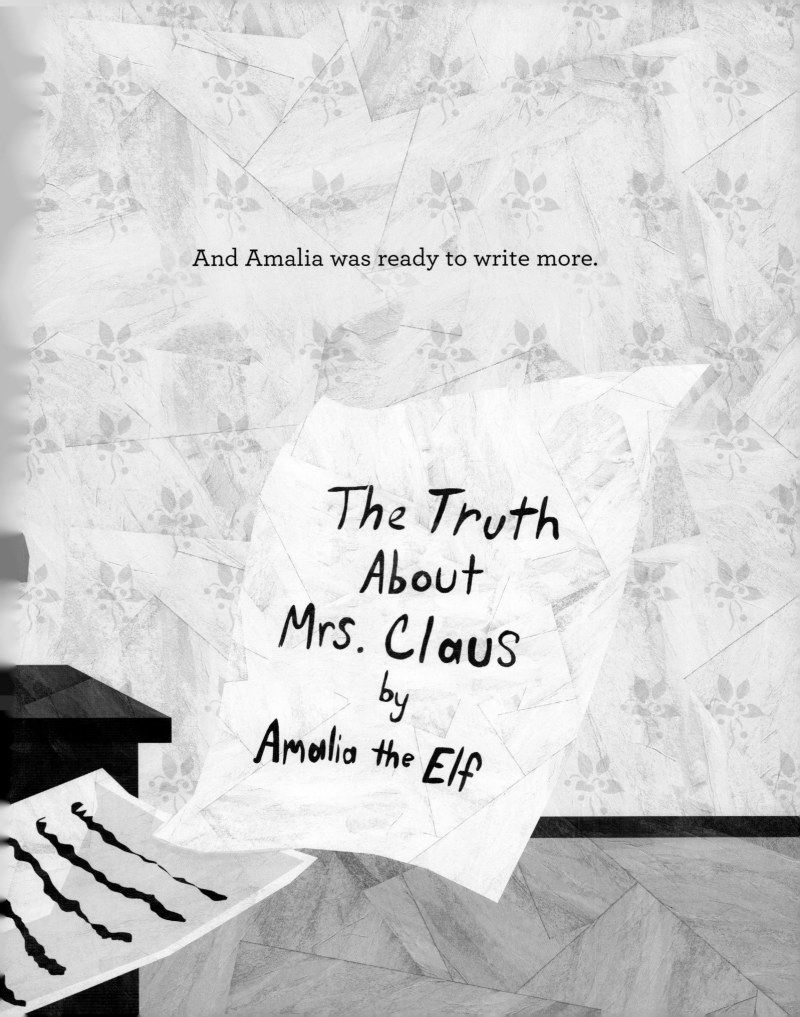

The Truth
About
Mrs. Claus
by
Amalia the Elf

AUTHOR'S NOTE

On Christmas morning a couple of years ago, one of my daughters asked what Mrs. Claus was doing while Santa delivered presents all over the world. Her question got me thinking: Why is it that we never really hear about Mrs. Claus? We don't even know her first name.

But what if Mrs. Claus's talents were just as important as Santa's? What if Christmas couldn't be the special day it is without her contribution? My daughter's question became a story about finding truth in your purpose while acknowledging the impact of traditions past. A story about intergenerational learning and growth, about finding your own way, even when it means reshaping other's expectations.

The Truth About Mrs. Claus reflects questions I had as a young person, and the encouragement and wisdom I received from my grandmother. For anyone, changing course, developing new interests, and challenging norms can feel scary at first. I was lucky to have my grandmother's support, and Amalia is lucky to have Mrs. Claus's. I hope every child who picks up this book has someone in their corner as they forge new paths ahead.